The Chase of Dreams

Parmeet Singh

Invincible Publishers

First published in India in 2019

ISBN: 978-93-89600-09-4

Registered Address: 201A, SAS Tower, Sector 38,

Gurgaon-122003

Printed at Thomson Press (India) LTD

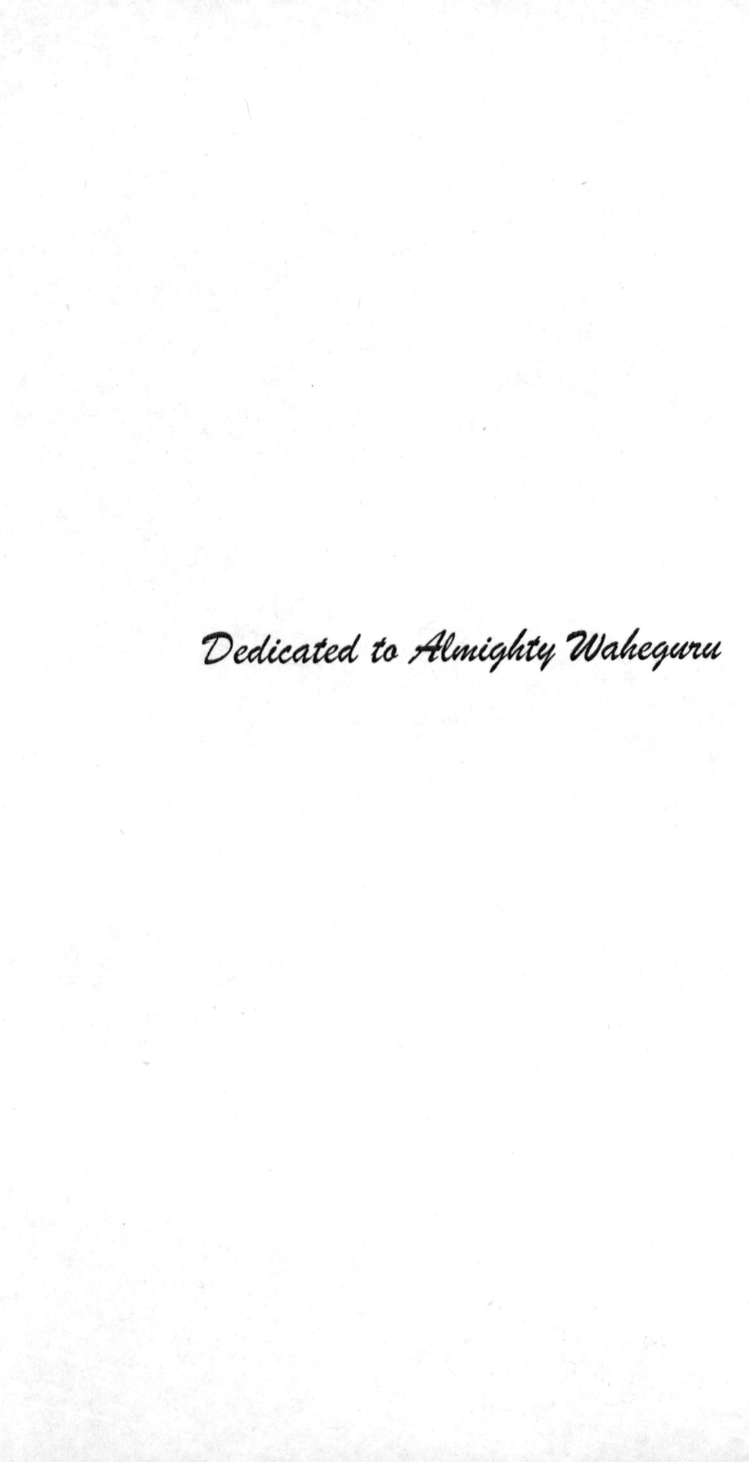

Dedicated to Almighty Waheguru

Acknowledgement

Writing of this novel has been a long journey. It has made me more confident in life & added a credential to my personality. It came through with the blessings of almighty God who showered me with the thoughts & power to initiate this novel. My first humble thanks goes to him.

I would like to thank my parents who always showed confidence in me & supported me in all my decisions. I would love to show my gratitude to the teachers of my school, Mukand Lal Public School & my college, Guru Gobind Singh College of Pharmacy, who played a major role in my development.

I would also like to thank the Rehan & Bhatti family for their love & support. Heartfelt thanks to Puneet Singla who encouraged me to give my ideas the form of a book. It would be unjust not to include the best people of my life in this – Kunal Sachdeva,

Manpreet Kaur, Sarthi Kochhar, Saurabh, Gundeep, Tarun & Dr Urvi Panchal who always showed faith in me.

Last but not the least, I would like to thank Invincible Publishers & Marketeers who gave me the platform to publish this novel.

Chapter 1

20th September 1990

What should have been a day to celcbrate is turning out to be gloomy reminder. It's the fifth marriage anniversary of Patrick Ray and Emma Ray but there are no celebrations in their house as the couple is still untouched with the happiness of a child. Despite many treatments, they harbor no hope. Ricky, the childhood friend of Patrick is back from his trip abroad with an address of Dr Jessica Williams. Ricky requests Patrick to consult with the doctor Williams who is a gynecologist for thirty years and is famous for treating the hopeless cases.

29th September 1990

Doctor gave Emma hopes of bearing a child; but with that also came strict advice regarding the dosage, as the drugs given were potent and needed to be handled carefully.

13th December 1990

Patrick after coming back from work rang the bell continuously and got terrified when Emma didn't respond. He managed to get in the house by breaking the backyard glass and was shocked to see Emma fainted in the living room. He rushed her to the hospital where doctors discovered the overdose of drug Clomiphene. Doctors also found that Emma was pregnant!

After two hours Emma gained consciousness. Doctor called them in his chamber and warned them regarding the dosage else there could be complications in delivery. Patrick and Emma went back home and Patrick decided to send Emma to her mother so that she gets proper care. Patrick had to leave within a week for his business trip.

8th July 1991

While Emma's mother was enjoying her post-lunch siesta, she was taken aback by Emma's loud cries of pain. Her mother lost no time in taking her to the hospital. Emma was immediately admitted in the hospital and in few hours she gave birth to a pre matured baby girl. Patrick after getting the news rushed towards the hospital. Both Patrick and Emma smiled at each other with wet eyes, the baby was a gift of Angels for them so they named her 'ANGEL RAY.'

2nd July 1995

Time has flown by quickly and little Angelis going to be of four years in six days. Patrick and Emma are planning a party at their place and have invited all the relatives and friends as per their list. Suddenly Patrick received a call from his client that he should reach the site within two days. Emma and little Angel felt let down and all the party preparations suddenly stalled. Patrick lifted their spirits and asked them to celebrate without him.

4th July 1995

Patrick is preparing to go, Emma is preparing food in kitchen while Angel is sleeping. Patrick wakes up Angel to bid her goodbye. Angel gave him a tight hug and started crying, 'Please Pa don't go!' **This was the first time Angel cried so badly, Patrick thought maybe she wanted him to be with her on her birthday, but still it was strange.** Somehow Emma calmed Angel and they said bye to Patrick. After 3 hours suddenly phone rang, Emma picked up the phone and from other side, **'Patrick is dead'** were the only words which Emma heard. Phone dropped from her hand and she was blank, Angel was saying something but Emma drowned in grief couldn't hear anything. Meanwhile Ricky, Patrick's best friend, called on Emma's mobile phone as he was not able to contact

Patrick. Angel picked up the phone but she was not able to speak. Sensing something wrong, Ricky and his wife arrived and saw Emma fainted. Ricky tried to ask Angel what happened. Angel said, 'Bad man hit Pa on his head near mall.' Ricky had no second thought as he rushed towards the mall and saw Patrick's body with a wound of bullet in his head!

5th July 1995

Patrick's funeral was solemnly performed at Saint Stephen church. **No one asked Ricky how he came to know about the place of that fatal incidence. Even Ricky never tried to ask Angel how she knew about Patrick's death.** With Patrick gone, life was not easy anymore for Emma and Angel. Emma was always busy in work now, her responsibilities were doubled and she was not able to give time to Angel. The cute smile of Angel was also fading away. Many a times she tried to tell something to her mother but she wasn't able to explain.

23rd October 1998

Angel is of seven years now. She was having a story telling competition a day later and so she was continuously asking for her mother's help. But as usual Emma was busy and Angel went to school with nothing prepared. In class when teacher Brianda asked Angel to present her story, she got nervous. Slowly she came in front of everyone and started narrating, **'One day a man with a bag came to market. He kept his bag near meat shop and went away. After sometime the bag exploded, everyone was running and crying...'** She got blanked out. Brianda asked her to sit down but her classmates were mercilessly teasing her. On returning home, Angel darted straight into her room and started crying. Her mother tried to talk to her but Angel didn't speak with her.

30th October 1998

Brianda was sitting in teacher's room when another teacher came to her and informed her regarding a bomb blast in their city. She turned the television on and was shocked to see that point of blast was a bag near butcher's shop. She was trying to think how a seven year old girl already knew about the incident. After two days Brianda's husband Smith came back after three weeks of his official visit, Brianda was excited to see her husband but she was not able to forget what happened in the last couple of days. She was relaxed and was enjoying the time, and after they had dinner and were in bed, Smith found her a bit uncomfortable. 'Something's missing in you babe,' he cajoled the wife. Brianda showed him a class group photo to Smith, pointed towards Angel and told him the complete story. Somehow he made Brianda comfortable and made love. Brianda slept but Smith couldn't. **He was a CIA agent but Brianda was not aware. As per Brianda he was a software engineer. This instance made Smith curious to know about Angel and her family.**

Next day he reported at CIA office and started investigation.

7th November 1998

Police arrested Emma Ray from her house soon after Angel left for the school. Emma was shocked and she was shouting, 'Why are you taking me? What have I done?'Police just took her to the police station and made her sit in the interrogation room. After five minutes Smith came and in a very harsh tone asked Emma, 'For whom you are working? Why you killed so many innocents?'

Emma was shocked and had no words to say. Smith went on, 'From where you got the bomb? Who else is there with you?'

'I Don't know what you are saying. What have I done, why I am here? Emma asked. At this moment two men came inside the cabin and one of them said 'You are accused to be a part of bomb blast incident that happened on 30th October in the market.'

'No, I don't know anything about it, I have done nothing!'

'Mrs. Ray, this is the intelligence report - Patrick Ray was supposed to deliver the bomb to the person who placed the bomb near the butcher's shop. But as he was shot by Andrew, the notorious gangster, you completed the task by supplying the bomb.'

'What the hell are you saying! Patrick was a reputed trader, he could never do such shit,' Emma replied back.

Smith felt that something was messed up. He felt that there is something which Emma was not aware of. Mean while a number of questions were asked to her by senior officers and the only answer she had was, 'I know nothing.'

After one hour the senior officers went out but they decided to keep Emma in custody for further investigation. Smith was standing outside the cabin and was watching Emma through the glass. Emma was continuously crying. Smith went inside and asked her politely, 'How you met Patrick?'

Emma spoke with tears in her eyes, 'I was working in a coffee shop, he often used to come there. He became a good friend of mine and after one year he proposed to me and we got married.' Smith offered her water and asked, 'Did you ever asked him what he does?'

'He told me that he and his friend Ricky were traders. After one year of our marriage Patrick and Ricky started to have some issues and they separated their business. For three months they didn't even meet when I called up Ricky for their patch-up which they had but they were never business partners again,' Emma replied.

Smith stood up and was going out when Emma said, 'My daughter is about to come from school, I need to be with her'. He said nothing and moved on. He directly went to the cabin of senior officers and tried to convince them that she knew nothing and they should release her. But seniors were not ready to do that, they thought Emma knew everything and she was the one who delivered the bomb. Smith demanded for the NARCO test and was able to convince them for that. Officers took permission from higher officials to conduct the NARCO test which could happen next day. Smith went to Emma and told her about the NARCO test, Emma got enraged and denied for the same. Smith politely told her that she was left with no choice and till that happens she is going to be in the custody. Emma was worried for Angel as she was about to leave from the school so she requested Smith to arrange a phone call so that she could send Angel to her nanny. Smith asked for the permission from his officers and arranged a phone call and Angel was sent safely to her nanny's home.

8th November 1995

Emma was taken to the forensic lab where her body test was done. After that under doctors' surveillance, Sodium Amytal was injected inside her body. Emma slipped into subconscious state within 10 minutes after which questions were repeatedly asked to her. Truth came in front of all and Emma was proved to be innocent and hence was soon released. Emma felt very low and was very disappointed after knowing the reality of her husband and she started to blame Patrick for all. Slowly she got depressed, was always angry on Angel and started to scold her for small things. Due to all this Angel was not able to go to the school for five days.

Unaware of what had happened, Brianda decided to visit Angel's home so as to know the reason for Angel's continued absence. When she reached there she was shocked to know all that happened with Emma. After thinking for five minutes Brianda said,' **I am sorry mam, I should have told you everything.'**

'Pardon me, but what you should have told me?

'Mam, a few weeks before there was a story telling competition and the story that Angel told happened exactly as bomb blast incidence. Angel knew that the bomb blast was to take place and when I asked her how she knew it she told me that she saw it in her dreams. I think mam you should talk to her and try to find out how exactly she knew all. Take care mam!'

One after other Emma was getting big surprises which were affecting her mental health. That night, she had a drink and went to sleep. Angel was also getting badly disturbed and her sleep was gone. She had stopped playing, was always lying on her bed and always thinking something. The next morning Emma was woken up by a loud sound of glass breaking. She ran towards kitchen and saw the cookies jar was broken and a piece of glass was pierced in Angel's foot. Blood was spread on the floor and sitting in a corner Angel was crying. Emma got emotional watching her – Angel was hungry and was trying to reach the cookie jar on the second shelf but the jar slipped from her hands and was broken. Emma hugged Angel and with wet eyes took her to the bed. She gave her first-aid, prepared nice breakfast and they had it on Angel's bed. Emma was trying to make Angel relax. She left Angel to her mother and went for work. Entire day only the words of Brianda were ringing in her mind. She stayed at office after her shift and was worried when suddenly an idea clicked and she rushed to the nearest library. She was trying to find whether such power of dreams exist or not? While searching she found some books which mentioned about a type of dream known as premonition dream, in which people later discover that the same incidence was happening to them which they had seen in their dream.

Emma got shocked as Angel related to this condition. On further research she came to know that a few drugs overdose lead to activation of Dorso lateral Prefrontal Cortex in the brain, due to which neurotransmitters get fully activated and a person gets the unusual power of dreaming. Emma was stunned when she found Clomiphene was listed in such drugs! This was the drug which had over the required dose during her pregnancy!!!

Everything was clear to her now how Angel had gotten that power. She thought if Angel's powers could be used for predicting the future so that the losses could be prevented. She also read about lucid dreaming - a dreaming condition in which a person is in sub-conscious stage and can tell what is being seen in the dreams. Such condition during sleep happens between 2am to 4am at night. After gathering all the information Emma came back to her mother's place and found that Angel was sleeping. Emma was very curious to use the information she had gathered and decided not to sleep that night. Now she was waiting for **2 AM…**

Chapter 2

It's 2 AM and Emma slowly enters the Angel's room, Angel is sleeping tight, Emma sits beside her and slowly speaks 'Hello Angel' and she got no response. Emma came more closer and speaks in Angel's ear, 'Hello Angel,' 'Hi' Angel responded very slowly. Emma got stunned and thought for the second thing to ask her. 'You know who I am?' 'No!'Emma got more confidence and the conversation began. 'I am your friend'. 'Ok,'

'Do you know my name'. 'No,' 'I am your Barbie doll hmm…' 'You are watching something' 'hmm…' 'What?' Angel turned another side, Emma thought maybe Angel get awakened. So she quit that time and went to other room, next morning when Angel waked up. Came to her mom and gave her a tight hug. Emma wanted to know whether Angel remembers that she had a talk with 'Barbie' She asked her. 'Hey princess how was your last night'.

'Nanny gave me burger'. 'And what else happened'. 'And I went to sleep then' suddenly nanny called Angel. 'Come on get ready for school, you are already late. One thing was clear to Emma that Angel didn't remember about the talk Emma had last night with her. In-office each and every minute Emma was thinking. That how she could engage Angel with her and know what the Angel is dreaming. That night also Emma didn't sleep and was waiting for the clock to strike 2am. Emma went to Angel's room, Angel was sleeping tight, slowly Emma asked Angel, 'Hello friend you remember me?'

'Barbie' this was something which made Emma anxious, now Emma could ask her something more… 'What are you doing? In the market'. 'Who else is there with you'. 'Mommy,'

'What is your mommy doing? 'Crying'

'Why your mommy is crying?' 'Man with knife'. 'What else that man is doing?' She got no reply, she tried to ask thrice. But no response came then, Emma got furious that something bad is going to happen with her. She went back and was not able to sleep.

The next day Emma took half day and went to pick up Angel from her school. Angel was delighted that today mommy is there for her and she took her to the market. Emma bought Angel an ice cream and was waiting for something to happen. After one hour also Emma didn't understand what she was expecting?

So finally she decided to go back home, Emma thought that earlier the incidents happened might be some co incidents, so that night she slept, for a couple of days Emma did the same so that no doubt was left and went to the market with Angel, but nothing happened. Five days had gone and Emma was now confident enough that nothing will happen now, next weekend Emma, Nanny and Angel went to a carnival they enjoyed a lot there. Nanny suddenly met a group of her old friends there and decided to spend some time with them so Angel and Emma decided to go back home. And after taking the car from parking. Emma and Angel decided to have meat balls that night, so they turned towards market. After purchasing meat from butcher's shop Angel insisted her mother for a candy and Emma bought, now when they were turning back to the car. Suddenly a man came with his face covered and a knife in his hand. 'Come on give me purse, do it fast give me your purse'. He snatched Angel 'Come on give me the purse quick, else your daughter is a dead girl'.

'Ok…Ok, you got it don't harm the child, here it is' suddenly a few men came from back and grabbed the thief from behind. And got control over him, one called the police. After 5 mins the nearest patrolling unit responded and took charge. Got everything controlled and let Emma go with Angel, she was crying, and Emma was totally blank. As soon as they reached home Emma found that. Angel got asleep slowly Emma put her in bed and went for a shower the market scenes. And Angel's dream talk were not letting here being calm, incident was so similar.

This day again Emma waited for 2 am, went to Angel's bed and whispered. 'Hi Angel, No response. 'Hi Angel, I am Barbie'.

'Hi'.

'What are you doing princess?'

'Nothing.' 'Are you watching something?'

'Yes'.

'What is it?'

'Carnival.' 'What is in old carnival lady?' 'What is she doing?' 'Lying!' Emma got curious but still whispered in her ear.

'Where is she lying?' 'In blood' Emma got blanked She asked Angel in cracking voice 'Who else is there?' Now there was no reply from Angel, Emma asked thrice but still no response. Emma got furious because her mother went on with her friends in carnival. And due to the thief incident she skipped to call her mother and also her mother didn't give a call, It's 2:30 am she has made 10 calls to her mother.

No call was received, also neither she had any contact of her mother's friends nor their address. That night Emma didn't slept, it was 7 am Emma's phone ranged and Emma picked up the call in hurry. 'Hello!'

'Hello darling, you have given me 10 calls is everything fine,' Emma was calm that her mother was fine. But she didn't tell her anything,

'Nothing mom I was worried where are you?' 'Oh dear! I am at my friend's place, we had fun last night'.

'Ok mom so when you are coming back.' She asked 'Not today we are going back to the carnival yester tomorrow we were not able to see the complete place'. Suddenly her friend called from the back to get into the car. 'Hey dear I'll call you back later my friends are in hurry take care'. 'Hey mom listen,' And suddenly the call got disconnected. Emma tried to call her back but Emma's phone ran out of signal. Emma got worried as she didn't even know that in how much time her mother is going reach the carnival. So she decided to pick Angel and leave for the carnival immediately within half an hour. She reached the carnival, left Angel in kids room and rushed towards the main place. She ran to find out her mother.

After taking a complete round of carnival worried Emma stood beside an ice cream shop. All of a sudden she saw her mother coming with her group Emma ran towards her mother gave her a tight hug and her mother asked 'What happened dear, is everything fine?' All of a sudden one of the old lady from her grandmother's group went to the juice bar nearby to have some juice. Suddenly short circuit happened in the grinder. And the blade broke up and pierced into her throat blood oozed and the old lady felt on the floor and died on the spot. Now the scene was the same which Angel told her mother and Emma realized that it wasn't her mother's death which Angel watched. A few days later after attending the funeral of her mother's friend Emma was curious to know that what next she can get from Angel. Because after each talk in the explanation given by Angel was increasing so Emma decided to continue the exercise daily this night Emma tried to have some more questions so that she is able to gather more information 'Hi Angel, How are you doing'?. 'Hi Barbie, This time Angel recognized her 'Where are you now Dear?'

'I am at my school' 'What is happening there?' Allen Angel's classmate asked, 'What is happening there?'

'A big dog'.

'What Angel, what is the big dog doing here?' There was no reply 'Angel come on baby tell me what is the dog doing to him?'

'He is biting Allen' 'My dear can you see date or time anywhere' again there was no reply. 'Please Angel concentrate try to see the time or date,' It's 1:25' 'Perfect dear from where you have seen the time?' 'Clock tower' 'Can you see the date anywhere?'

'No' 'Please dear try to see it,' Angel turned another side 'Angel?' 'Can you hear me now' No answer came from her this time Emma was a bit happy because Angel showed improvement in telling the situation but was also worried for Allen. Next morning while driving Angel to her school Emma was trying to get some info from Angel regarding Allen and his family so that she could prevent the incident, 'Hey honey! We never talked about your friends, tell me their names'.

'I have two friends mom Stacy, and Bincy.'

'How many boys are there in your class?' 'I don't know!' 'No boy is your friend?' 'No!' It was getting difficult for Emma to know about Allen. Soon they reached school Emma dropped Angel and was watching her until she entered the building, all of a sudden she saw that a group of boys came near her and one of them pulled Angel's pony and ran away. Angel stood there and started crying, as Emma was there she came out of the car and ran towards Angel angry Emma asked Angel to come into school with her, and they are going to complain about the incident. They reached Angel's class Brianda was there in the class Emma told her about the incident. Brianda asked Angel the name of the boy who teased her 'Allen pulled my pony!' And Angel started crying again. Brianda gave a hug to Angel and assured Emma that she will complain to his mother but Emma insisted to meet Allen's mother and in her mind it was the only chance to meet Allen's mother.

It was not that she wanted to complain but also wanted to make her aware of the incident, Brianda called up Allen's mother and asked her to come soon. Jane (Allen's mom) was very arrogant, as she reached school before letting Emma meet her Brianda talked to her regarding the pony pulling incident. Jane got angry and believed that her son could never do such a thing, Brianda then sent Emma inside before she could say anything. Jane started 'Hello Mrs…'

'Emma, my name is Emma'. 'Whatever it is, my son is an obedient and polite boy, he cannot make such mischief'. 'Mrs Jane, I have seen myself Allen teasing my girl, but I have some other concern today'.

'Ahh...Your girl might have done something, so in return she got it, never try to blame my son again,' Jane turned around and left the room. Emma got annoyed of her behavior. And she went out of the room, she held the arm of Jane.

'Listen, I just wanted to tell something related your son related to his safety'. 'Excuse me are you trying to threaten my child, I'll call the police, come Allen'. Jane asked Brianda to take Allen along with her. All of a sudden Emma looked at her wrist watch it was 1:20pm she rushed towards the gate of the school. As soon as she reached there she saw a girl walking by the side with her dog. And Jane along with Allen were waiting for their car to arrive at a distance. Now it was 1:25 pm the time Angel told for the accident also the girl with dog was approaching towards Jane and Allen, by the time dog could be near Allen, their car approached, Jane and Allen got into the car and moved on…Encounter didn't happened…Emma got that it was some other day the incident to be happened. For a next few days Emma came everyday to Angel's school for half an hour (1pm to 1:30pm) but the incidence didn't happened. After 5 days there was an immediate work to be completed by Emma, and she couldn't go to Angel's school that evening Emma came back home late. As in her absence Grandma picked Angel from her school, she told Emma that near Angel's school a boy was badly bitten by a dog, her mother was buying him an ice cream. A man walked through them with a dog (Pit bull).

The little guy was teasing the dog all of a sudden the dog lost the control and bit him on his leg. The boy got badly injured and is in hospital now. Emma was quiet outside but in her mind many things were running so she decided to tell her mother about Angel's power of dreams. After listening to Emma she got a big shock for long time they both were silent, suddenly Angel came running to her mom and asked her to give something to eat.

Emma went on to kitchen to prepare dinner and granny looked after Angel, after they had dinner Angel went to sleep and Emma was doing some of her office work granny came to her and told her about one of her friend's daughter who was an expert in yoga and meditation. She asked Emma to meet her once if she could help in a way or other, that time Emma agreed to her mom but didn't want to go there as she thought that being a mother she could only be the best trainer for Angel.

Chapter 3

As the time passed Angel started giving more response, due to the regular exercise Angel was able to look around in her dream. She was able to read the names of shops. Time, date even if the place was known to her she was able to tell that as well. Its, April 2008, Angel is now of 18 years and her high schools are over, she is going to start her higher studies now, day before going to college Emma had the routine exercise at 2 am 'Hi Angel' 'Hi Barbie, so what's Angel watching right now.'

'I am in a cab.'

'So where are you going.'

'I Don't know.'

'What's there around you?'

'It's Coca-Cola warehouse I am passing by.'

'Who's there with you?' 'I don't know a guy is there.'

Suddenly Angel started giving some strange expressions and Emma noticed that 'What is happening, baby?

It's a strange way; boy has pulled out a gun,

I am afraid'.

'Baby can you see the date and time?'

'No, nothing is there to see.'

'Dear try to see something, please.'

'Guy is holding a phone time is 11:23 am date is 9th April' Emma got frightened because it was the same date, that means for this day Emma had to drop Angel by her only. Now in the morning, Angel was ready for the college and was surprised to see that Emma was already ready to go. Emma told Angel that today she was going towards her college and will drop her, Angel agreed and requested her mom to wait for a while. As her friend, Julia was also about to come, after 15 minutes Julia came, and they left the house, it was 10:05 am after 1 km only the car stopped.

The catalytic converter got choked, Emma called her friend who lived nearby. As it was taking time Julia asked Emma to go in a taxi suddenly Emma gave a weird reaction and said no to them. After waiting for sometime Julia insisted again to go now Angel also asked her mom to do the same. Emma shouted at her 'When I am saying not to go in-cab, then it's a clear no wait for the moment.' Angel got annoyed and replied back

'What's wrong with you, the car is not working, and we are getting late that's why we are asking to go, we are going in-cab now, come Julia,' Emma stopped them from going and got very angry on Angel, all of a sudden a car came and stopped nearby them. It was Steve in the car which was the old friend of Julia, he came out and asked 'What happened, is everything alright? 'Julia told her the complete incidence. And Steve offered them to drop to the college. Emma could not resist them and let both the girls go with Steve, after a few minutes Emma's friend came.

Emma asked him to have his car keys. She got his car keys and just went on to the college, it was exactly 11:43 am when Emma reached the college, after a few moments Julia along with the Steve arrived Emma asked Julia that where Angel was. Julia got afraid and told Emma that Steve had some important work and it was taking some time. And Angel hurried for the college and she took a cab. She said that Angel might already have reached college, Emma tried to call Angel but her phone was not reachable. Emma rushed inside college. But she got to know that Angel was not there yet, afraid

Emma started shouting at Julia, all of a sudden Angel arrived and asked Emma ‘ What happened, mom?’

‘Oh dear, where were you are you fine where The boy who had gun Is?’

‘Mom I am alright, and which gun?’

‘Listen, Angel, I am no fool, my friend passed by your cab, and he saw a boy having the gun, tell me what happened (shouted).’ The boy standing behind Angel took out the gun and said,

‘You are looking for this, it’s a lighter.’ Everyone standing there started laughing,’

‘I am Alex I was in the cab with your daughter, and this is the gun I had’ Angel felt embarrassed and ran inside the college. Emma silently walked away, Angel in break time approached Alex and felt sorry for her mom’s behavior. And after that they became friends. Emma went on to her work, one thing was there in her mind that now Angel is not at all aware of her dreams. She now decided that she will try to make Angel aware of her powers. In the evening, Angel came back home and saw Emma preparing Angel's favorite food. Angel being angry went to her room without talking to Emma. She noticed that Angel is home, she went to her room to have some talk, but Angel shouted at her,' Mom, I don't want to talk to you please leave.' 'Honey it's your favorite food I have prepared for you.'

'Thanks mom, you already gave me my favorite in the college, I need nothing now.' Sadly Emma came back to kitchen and placed everything in kitchen and waited for 2 am. At 2 am Emma approached Angel's room, she heard some voice, Angel was talking to someone Emma slightly open the door and saw Angel was talking to someone on the phone, suddenly Angel saw that her mom was in the room,' Honey you didn't sleep?' Angel in a surprised voice,

'Actually I was talking to Julia for some assignment.'

'Sleep timely sweetheart, you have to wake up in the morning.' Emma went to her room this day she was worried as she was not knowing what next is going to happen. Next morning Emma wake up at 9:30 AM, she rushed to Angel's room but she was not there, Emma just picked up her phone to call Angel, Granny came out of her room and told Emma that Angel already left for the college. Emma got bit disappointed and wanted to see Angel so she got ready and was just leaving for Angel's college suddenly granny asked Emma to drop her at her friend's place. Emma did so and then again was going to Angel's college, before reaching there she got a call from her boss to reach office soon.

Emma sadly went to office whole day she was just thinking of Angel's safety at nearby 3:45pm Emma got a call from an unknown number it was a call from granny's friend, granny was admitted to the hospital. Emma rushed towards hospital and saw that due to kidneys failure and infection Granny was at her last moments, Emma went into ICU hold granny's hand and was trying to have some talks with her. Granny said just one thing 'Angel is a special child but unaware of it, this could be harmful, take care of her.' and after 5 minutes granny passed away. Emma was broken and depressed, Angel came back home at 6 pm and got the news, but Angel was not much effected. The next day after funeral when Emma and Angel came back home Emma tried to have a talk with Angel but she was not interested and went into her room. Emma had only one thing in her mind that if Angel would have slept on time she could get clue of the incident and could try to save granny. That day also Emma got into Angel's room at 2 am, but she was again talking to someone.

Emma went back to her room and spent whole night crying. A week after, Emma got stabled and was back to life. But her conversation with Angel was almost nothing. Day by day difference between Angel and Emma increased. Daily Angel use to talk someone late night. And Emma got to know nothing way ahead, at the weekend Emma was home and was trying some ways to engage Angel with her. She decorated Angel's room prepared food and was waiting for Angel to come, Emma waited for long and slept in Angel's room, at 1:30 am doorbell rang. Emma opened the door and was shocked to see Angel drunk, even she was not able to walk properly.

Emma held her arm and tried to balance her also she saw a car moved from her gate as soon as Emma helped Angel. it was the one with whom Angel was, Emma took Angel to her bed, removed her shoes and tried to make her comfortable, when Emma was leaving Angel's room she realized that it was 2 am after so long she had a chance to know that what is going to happen,' Hi Angel,' no-reply came she tried again,' Honey can you hear me,' 'Barbie?'

Emma got excited, 'Yes, its Barbie, where are you, my child,'

'I am with him.'

'With whom?'

'Alex,'

'Where are you both?'

'At his home, he is so handsome,' 'What are you both doing there?' 'He proposed me, he wanna marry me,' Emma got blank, even she forgot to ask for the time or date or any other information. She got one thing that it was Alex with whom Angel talks late night. Emma didn't sleep that night but also she had no thoughts but a negative feeling. The next day she decided that she will meet Alex and will try to find out if he was good for Angel or not, Angel woke up with hangover and found that Emma was now angry and was not at all talking to her.

Angel didn't bothered she prepared coffee for herself, got ready and went out for the college.

Emma intentionally showed her anger. Now she left home and moved towards Angel's college. As expected Emma saw Angel with Alex and approached them. Angel shouted at Emma,' Mom why are you here?'

'I wanted to have a word with gentleman' Alex stepped forward to talk but Angel hold his hand and said,'

'Please mom do not embarrass us,' and with Alex Angel moved ahead, Emma was feeling very down, with wet eyes she went away for the work. That night Emma got drunk and slept. Next morning Emma saw flowers on the table. She understood that Alex presented her the flowers but was quiet, for the next 3 days Angel and Emma had no conversation even Emma didn't try to come to Angel at 2 am. After 3 days Angel came to Emma and told her that there was a nature camp from her college for a week so she would be going there and as they have to leave early morning.

She is going to sleep, Emma took this as an opportunity to know something. She went on to Angel's room at 2 am and started the conversation,' Hi Angel.' No response came from her side. After Emma called her 3 times she got a response,' Hi You remember me, honey,' 'No,' 'I am Barbie, your friend.' 'Barbie,' Emma came to know one thing that day as it was a huge gap that Emma wasn't able to do the exercise Angel was not properly giving the responses but all of a sudden Angel started giving some strange expressions, Emma Asked,' Angel what happened where are you…'

'A dark room, my hands are tied my mouth is tied,'

Why honey, can you see something else?' 'No…'

'He wants to kill me, he will kill me,' and after saying these things, Angel got normal and went into deep sleep. Emma tried to talk more but was of no use, now Emma was afraid, again for the whole night Emma was not able to sleep. She was clear that at any cost she won't let Angel go on the camp. It was 5 am Angel woke up so as to get ready, as soon as she went to the kitchen she saw juice and sandwiches were ready for her with a love you note. But Angel knew that Emma has prepared it for her she was about to have it but all of a sudden she got a call, Alex was standing outside her home to pick her up.

Angel rushed to him, and they went on, Emma's plan failed, in juice hypnotic drug was being added by her. And she was there in another room. Now worried Emma tried to chase them in car but was not able to do so, Emma moved her car towards Angel's college after reaching there she saw no one was there. She saw only few athletes she tried to ask them regarding the children who went for the camp, but they knew nothing, Emma got afraid and started crying after some time. A boy approached her and told her that she could get some information from the coach who was about to reach after 10 minutes coach arrived. And Emma got horrified after hearing that the college never arranged such type of camp.

Emma rushed towards the police station. There she got to know that the officer on duty was yet to arrive so she had to wait for a while suddenly Smith arrived there. Smith remembers Emma as he interrogated her for bomb blast case years ago. He approached her and asked her if everything was fine, Emma told him that Angel told her she is going to a camp but now she know that there was no such camp arranged and Emma was worried for Angel's safety. Smith helped her, took some details of Angel and requested special team to track Angel's location through her phone. After an hour Smith got a call with the location of Angel, with a team of 5 members Smith left for the location. Location was of an old factory which was not in the function, all the officers got into the position. And they saw that 4 boys were standing around and Alex was standing with the gun pointed at Angel's head.

Chapter 4

After the officers saw that gun was pointed at Angel. They got into the move, the shooter shot right on the hand of Alex due to which his gun dropped. And the police was able to rescue Angel. As soon as they reached police station after taking statement of Angel they released her to go along with Emma, but she insisted on knowing why Alex did so. Smith took a special permission and they could see on the screen the interrogation of Alex. From there a shocking truth revealed, Alex told that his father was one of the business partner of Patrick (Angel's father), they both were involved with drugs and ammunition trading.

One day his father discovered that Patrick was betraying him and for the clarification he went to have a word with Patrick, the talk turned violent and Patrick killed his father, Andrew was the younger brother of his father and in rage Andrew shot Patrick dead, further he said that when the lighter gun incident happened and when Angel came to me for the apologies, ever since he started liking her.

One day when Angel told him her father's name he got blanked because that was the name his mother told him was the murderer of his father. So he decided to avenge his father so he made a plan and everything was going as per the plan but all of a sudden police came and all I had planned was finished, after knowing this Angel got stunned, Emma took her to the home made tried to make her comfortable but she was quiet now, somehow Emma managed to convince Angel to had dinner with her, Emma planned to tell Angel about her powers as it was the right time,' Sweetie, there is something I wanted to tell you,' 'Yes mom.'

'I already knew that what was going to happen that's why I was insisting you to not to go,'

'I didn't understand mom how did you know that?' Then Emma started telling her regarding the exercise she used to do when Angel was in a deep sleep and also to make her believe. Emma told her the related incidents. Angel got emotional not because of anything else, but because of the sacrifice, her mother did for all these years and also because of her care. Angel hugged Emma and just started crying, Emma made her calm down and said, 'You can increase your powers, and I will help you in doing that just I need is your cooperation,' Angel agreed to it, and from the same day they started practice, 2 am Emma use to call out, and Angel replied her questions, and the next morning Emma use to ask questions regarding last night dreams. Slowly with practice Angel started remembering her dreams and also could see every point in her dreams.

Now she could reveal the incident and get prepared for it, one thing was widespread, Emma and Angel tried a lot to save someone or to change the incident but by one way or other whatever was there in Angel's dream would happen exactly. By the time Both realized that they could get ready only to face the incident. Angel has completed her graduation and is doing job in a domestic company.

Now life was through and smooth until she met Ryan, he was Angel's new boss, and after some time they started liking each other. Angel shared this with her mom. Also Emma was positive about this man, after a few days, Emma noticed in Angel's dream that they would get married. So Emma let Angel be with him, after 2-year relationship they decided to get married. Its 13th October 2016, Angel is of 26 years the very next day she was to get married, Emma didn't do the 2 am exercise .14th October 2016 Ryan and Angel got married, day before leaving home mom-daughter decided to be awake whole night and talk, again the 2am exercise was not done, the next day Ryan and Angel were about to leave. Emma told Angel about the procedure of practice, and now as they both won't be together. Angel has to practice herself. They took leave for honeymoon. for a week they were for the honeymoon and Angel couldn't practice, now it was 9 days exercise not done. When they came back and just entered their home they receive a call.

It was from the neighborhood, Emma passed away, Angel was in shock, on the funeral also she was just remembering her talks. Again the two nights spent and she was not able to sleep, next day Ryan went to work and asked Angel to take rest. After two hours Angel heard a voice calling her, she got afraid, she stood up to see from where the voice was coming. When she went towards her room. She went blank, she saw Emma sitting in her room. Angel started crying and gave her a hug, Emma made Angel comfortable, 'Baby, it's the wheel of life everyone has to go, but I am alive in you, you just focus on yourself, you are given a beautiful gift by the God, keep practicing. I know it's tough for you to do it alone, but now you have to do it,'

'Mom, I haven't slept yet I am tired, can I sleep on your lap.'

'Come my doll,' Ryan came back from the office at 7:00pm and found that Angel was sleeping. He made her awake. Angel woke up and started finding Emma, but she was not there then Angel told her that she saw her mom and she made her sleep. Ryan took Angel to the bedroom and told her that her mom was in her mind no in real and now she has to accept it. Angel got calm and went on to kitchen, prepared food for them, and went on to bed.

That night she saw some dream, but when she woke up she didn't revive the dream. She got tensed that now she won't be able to use her power. Days went, and every day she was trying to revive her dream but always failed. One morning she woke up frightened and that day she revived the dream, she saw that she was in the hospital and was crying loudly. She was not able to understand what was going to happen. Earlier she thought to share this with Ryan, but then she decided to keep it to herself.

Deep inside she was worried a lot and started getting more conscious in routine work, she thought that she might meet an accident and that's why got the dream of getting hospitalized. A month has gone, but nothing happened. Suddenly she realized that she has missed her periods, she went on for the pregnancy test, it was positive. Ryan and Angel were expecting a baby, by eve she gave this news to Ryan he was delighted, and they decided to celebrate the news with everyone at weekend.

They had a grand party every friend and relative were invited, and at that time Angel was missing Emma a lot, after party when Ryan and Angel went on to the home and were about to go to bed . Angel again felt that some voice was coming from kitchen. Angel moved towards kitchen and saw Emma. Angel ran towards her and told about the baby to come, Emma kissed Angel's forehead and made her comfortable, she guided her that in happiness, do not forget that you are losing your power.

You need to meditate, you need to maintain your inner peace then only you would be able to focus on the dreams you see and remember them, then Emma gave a tight hug to Angel and Angel slept there only. That night she slept calmly. The next morning when Ryan found Angel missing in the bed. He got worried and was trying to find her in every room. Suddenly he discovered Angel sleeping on the chair, he woke her up and asked why was she sleeping there. Angel was behaving very confused.

She urged to go to the washroom and went there. Angel found that she remembered the dream, she saw that Ryan was sitting with a girl in a restaurant and was sitting very close, this time Angel had a keen watch on the dream, she was able to see where exactly were they sitting. She came out and reached the room Ryan was getting ready to go somewhere.

Angel asked him where was he going, he said that he is going to meet an old friend. Angel asked him if she could also join them, but Ryan refused. Angel got angry and decided to catch him, she followed him and saw he was meeting the same girl.

They hug and ordered something, were sitting holding each other's hand, Angel couldn't stop herself, she went to them banged the table, 'Oh so this is your old friend meeting right, you are cheating on me,'

'Are you out of your mind,'

'Yes I am, how could you do this to me.' Seeing this that girl jumped in,

'My name is Sophie, Ryan, me and my husband Cory were in the same batch in college, please do not misunderstand, my husband is about to join us,'

'Then why you didn't let me join you,'

'We were planning a surprise for you, they were not able to make it for the party we had. So I was planning a different thing for you,' they made Angel comfortable. Angel was happy that she was not cheated but was feeling bad as she was not able to see complete details in the dream.

She got to understand that why she got an advice from Emma for meditation, after some time Cory joined them and together they told that Cory and Sophie were also expecting the baby. They all decided to be in a regular touch now and they invited them for dinner. Angel was very clear now. She started meditation, also found some yoga exercises on internet, to increase the focus. A month practice made a difference. She was now again able to focus on the dreams, 26th August2016, Angel gave birth to a baby boy, and 1st September2016 Sophie and Cory were also blessed with baby boy.

Joy for both the couples was on top of the sky, for the weekend, i.e. 3rdth September 2016, they decided to throw a party. So for that they started making all the arrangements, on the big day both couples decided to name their babies. Angel and Ryan named their boy Shown Cory and Sophie named their boy Tyson two days after the party, Angel got a dream, she saw that Ryan and Cory were at a shop and all of a sudden few men with guns got into the shop and started asking for money.

Ryan tries to escape, but one of the robbers shot him, Angel tried to see the date, but she was able to see a blurred view of a digital clock. It was confusing that whether the date was 9/10/2016 or 10/9/2016, now Angel decided to tell Ryan regarding the dream and her power to see the future events in dreams. She thought that Ryan will understand her and will be aware of every fact across him. She found that Ryan was not at home. She called him and found that he went on for some work for 2 weeks.

Cory and Sophie would be at there place till he comes back, after two hours they both were at Angel's home. For next few days, they had perfect time and were enjoying. By this time Angel again stopped meditating, till next 2 nights she didn't get any other dream. Also Angel was eagerly waiting for Ryan to come back from work. On 3rd night Angel got a dream. That a guy with a mask having a knife got into their house and hold Sophie with knife on her neck. Angel was not able to see anything else the next day. Angel was very aware and was having a keen watch over whole house, this day nothing happened, Angel felt strange. She thought that the same thing will happen the next day, the next day also nothing happened. Next morning Angel heard scream of Sophie.

She got up and got the idea that her dream was getting true, she ran towards cupboard took the gun and ran towards hall, there she got that Spohie, cut her finger and that's why she screamed, Angel got blank, Sophie came and made her calm down, gave her water and went to other room to understand first aid for her after 10 minutes Angel felt strange because first aid box was on the table which takes only 3 to 4 minutes to make. She went into the room and was stubborn to see that a guy was holding Sophie's mouth and from another hand, he kept knife on her neck. He asked Angel to step back else he will kill Sophie, Angel took two steps back, with good reflex she took a pot kept on table and threw towards the guy.

That person got afraid and released Sophie, showed up his face, he was Ryan. It was a prank played by him. Both Sophie and Angel started crying, this prank turned out into a big issue when Sophie told this to Cory, Cory and Ryan had an argument and Cory took back Sophie to home, Angel was also upset, so Ryan decided to take her and Shown for an outing but all of a sudden she realize that it was 9th September and now she knew that for next day Cory and Ryan won't be meeting so the action is going to happen on 9th October, so she decided to tell Ryan regarding that on next day after the Trip...

Chapter 5

10th October 2016, Ryan, Angel and Shown went to the countryside for fun, Ryan left Shown and Angel to enjoy and left to take some refreshment for them, there was only one store there, and Ryan went there and saw that Cory was already there it was a total co incidence. Sophie was there with him, she tried for their patch up and they were back again. Cory asked Sophie to leave and meet Angel, till then they both will buy some snacks for them, Sophie along with Tyson went on to the place where Angel and Shown were already there. Angel got surprised, also got shocked. Soon as Sophie told that she was successfully able to bring Cory and Ryan back and they both were at the store, this reminded her about the dream, she got worried and ran towards store, also many other people were running away from the store, she got frightened, as soon as she reached there she saw that Cory was carrying Ryan's head on his lap and Ryan was shot dead, Angel broke down with grief, suddenly she got unconscious, Cory and Sophie looked after her , as soon as she gained conscious she just held Ryan's body and was continuously crying, Sophie handed Shown to Angel and said that for the sake of this baby you have to be strong Angel looked at Shown and kissed on his forehead, meanwhile police arrived and started with investigation Cory told police that a few men broke into the store and pointed the gun towards the owner and warned him if he won't give him the money he will shoot, Ryan and Cory just tried to protest they shot Ryan and when they realized that he is dead they ran away, when police took Ryan's body for the further processing, Angel was just broken and had only one thing in mind that why she delayed telling Ryan that she knew it and also she could prevent the incident.

After 1 day they got Ryan's body for the funeral ceremony which took place after that day, now the only reason of Angel's life was shown. He was the only one she had, she decided to live and move on for her son, but inside she was just blank and was accusing herself of the incidence, she started taking her power as curse, now she never wanted to have that power. But it was a '**Chase of dreams**' towards her. After a few days she decided to have a job again to support her child, for babysitting she requested Sophie because she was the only one whom she could trust. Angel got the job in the bread-making company as marketing executive. Day and night she tried to make her busy in the job, but every minute she mourned for Ryan. It was about a week, she followed only one routine.

Morning to the evening at work and just at night she uses to go back to Shown and every time she hugs Shown she felt Ryan is with her, night after a week she got a dream. This time she saw that Emma was sitting beside her bed she gave a tight hug and started crying, Angel shared with Emma the bunch of incidences happened with her, one thing she noticed was that Emma was worried, she asked Emma, 'Mom, what happened, for the first time I can see so much worry on your face.'.

'My child, I am worried not because of the incidence took place but for your negligence towards your power'.

'Mom please, that is a curse, not a power, it snatched everything from me, it ruined my life'.

'That's why I am worried, today I am here to warn you, be aware, many things in future are there, even worse, use your power that is the only way for you to survive.' Suddenly Angel woke up by the cry of Shown, she remembered the whole dream,

this was warning she took very seriously, she decided to do the meditation exercise and concentration building exercises on the regular bases before going to work, life thereafter was now stable, every Sunday Cory and Sophie along with their kid used to visit Angel, day after day Angel's stress started getting visible on her face.

Angel got very thin and had dark circles under her eyes, Sophie suggested her to take care else soon she will fall ill and then how she would be able to take care of Shawn. Also, Sophie and Cory insisted Angel to for a road trip next weekend, Angel got agreed. The following day she woke up early to do some exercises, but she was not willing to do concentration exercises, after two days. When she was recollecting all the old photographs she saw pic of Emma, all of a sudden she remembered of the dream where Emma told her to retain her power.

Angel thought that there might be some important incident to happen in future. That's why she got the indication, unwillingly. But Angel started meditating, night before the road trip, Angel got to see a dream, she could watch it in parts. The first scene she saw was the food store near the road, second scene Cory driving the car. Sophie and Angel holding babies, all of a sudden car bangs. The next scene Angel is sitting on the road holding baby in hand and baby was not moving. When she was about to see the face of the child.

Shawn started crying, and Angel woke up, she already hates that Dreaming and now she saw this horrifying dream, she got tensed and was about to call Sophie to refuse for the road trip, but all of a sudden. Doorbell ranged, she opened the door, Sophie, Cory and Tyson were there on the door. They were very excited about the trip, Angel tried to refuse, but they insisted. That dream was there in her mind while getting ready also she thought that somehow she could deviate the route, they left from home at 10:45 am, while sitting in car Angel was watching routes on her phone map, she saw a deviation from the route they were following to reach the point.

Angel insisted them to go from that route, when Cory agreed, Angel felt relaxed, after going on that route for 15 miles, they saw that route was closed due to an accident, they had to go back and follow the same old way, this made Angel worried, she thought that if she holds Tyson and give Shown to Sophie. Then Shown might survive and she did so. When they were back to the old route. Angel closed her eyes and was waiting for the action. When she opened her eyes, the food store she saw in the dream just passed through them, and nothing happened.

Angel got shocked, they completed the trip everyone enjoyed, but Angel was just thinking one thing that the incident didn't happen now it is going to be some other day. One week after that trip went off, that weekend Angel decided to go to market with Shown for some shopping when they were getting back to their home. Their car broke down, she called the mechanic and all of a sudden police reached there and asked if she needed any help.

Angel heard her name called out by someone, it was Cory in his car. He came out and asked Angel why she was there. After knowing the incidence, he insisted her to go along also mechanic reached there and told her that it will take at least 2 hours to repair. And he will drop her car to the home. So Angel along with Shown went on with Cory, she asked about Sophie. Cory told her that they are going to pick Sophie and Tyson from the saloon. They reached there, and Sophie was happy to see her. Then she said Cory that she just got a call from her brother and he is coming to visit them, so they need to go to the airport to pick him, so they all went on.

After some distance, they got a short cut lane for the destination and Cory took the car on that short cut. As soon as they entered highway Angel saw that it was the same road on which she saw the accident. Before she could say anything an uncontrolled high-speed car crashed into them, it caused huge damage to both the cars, two men from the store nearby came there to help them, they were able to rescue all of them out from the car. Cory's ribs were broken, Sophie got an injury on her head. Tyson was safe and was crying loudly. Angel didn't even get a scar on her body but one thing which was scary. Shown was not moving at all, Angel tried to shake him by trying to push him on the chest but it was of no use, a man who came for the help from store tried to give mouth to mouth resuscitation but he failed, Angel went into shock after watching this and got unconscious, everyone got scared, by the time Ambulance reached there and inside the ambulance Shown was given the Cardioversion, it was all god's grace that Shown's heart started beating again, but Angel was still unconscious, when they reached hospital, doctors declared

Angel in coma, Sophie and Cory felt very sad, and with wet eyes they saw Shown in other room, doctors said that the child was fine, but he won't be able to hear and speak due to accidental shock, and now they could take him back, everyone around there suggested Sophie and Cory to take Shown in their custody and they did so. After completion of all the legal formalities now Sophie and Cory were legal guardians of Shown. Its **3rd September 2035,** 19 years have passed since the accident, doctors were just doing the regular checkup all of a sudden doctor noticed that Angel's hand was showing some movement. The whole team gathered to see and started paying more attention after a week Angel regained conscious and first word she said was 'Shown'.

A man came inside saw her and asked doctor that when she could get discharged, doctor told that it could take either a month or 2, Angel thought that he was Shown, she tried to call him but her voice was not properly audible, nurse asked her to do rest, after 5 days doctors tried to make Angel walk and after a month's exercise she was able to walk, in between she continuously asked everyone to call his son but nobody paid attention and just asked her to be calm, after 2 and a half month nurse came to Angel and told Angel that she will get discharged today from hospital you may move to doctor's chamber, when she reached there she saw the same man which she thought that was Shown, she got near to him and gave him a tight hug and was just saying 'Shown my child' doctor told her that he was not her son, his name was Mr. James, manager of 'Care NGO' who took care of those people who were not having any relative, Angel all of a sudden started crying by just saying 'My son' she remembered the last thing was her son Shown dead in her hands, with discharge forms Angel was free from hospital, and Mr James took her to the social club where all the helpless people could live together and could be taken care of. Also, Mr James told her that the last people who visited her were Sophie and Cory 5 years before.

He asked her that they could search for them if she wanted, Angel felt bad that since 5 years no one has come to see her so now she also doesn't want them, as soon as they reached society club. Mr James introduced her to everyone as the new family member. Angel was shocked to see that there were many mid-aged and old aged people living there, all of them were either those who were homeless or those who do not have any relative alive. Everyone welcomed her and made her comfortable, introduction with everyone took long time, and at the dinner table everyone asked Angel to tell them about her life. While reaching the accident part of her life she broke down. Then everyone came together and made her comfortable and made her feel like home, the next day Aunty Shania told Angel that we being family here support each other and the house as well if she wants to do job then any one of them could help her. Then Angel noticed that many of the members go for the job and others take care of home. Angel thought something and started searching for the job, after a week she got a job in a general store on cash counter, on the first day she went to store andLily, who was already working there, she trained her will all the processes regarding billing etc. Also she stood beside her that day to help her out in the processes, the day went well, at the end of the day. Angel invited Lily for a cup of coffee to thank her for the help she did after she got back to the home she was thrilled and shared her experience with Aunty Shania, everyone had food together. And Angel went back to the bed, as soon as she got asleep, she saw a dream. There were a hardware store and a teenage boy arranging the stuff and from behind. Lily came and gave him a hug…

Chapter 6

The next morning Angel woke up and she remembered the dream, but it was not much special, she got ready for work, had breakfast and went on, she entered the store and Lily and Angel had friendly eye contact. Lily showed her the watch symbolising that she was late. And signed her to reach to the counter fast. Angel changed her uniform and got on the billing counter, at the time of lunch she sat with Lily, Lily asked her,' How you got late today?'

'It was a traffic issue'.

'You need to be on time boss is strict'.

'I'll take care of it,' Angel asked Lily,' Tell me something about your life?'

'Okay, I am from Florida, my dad is a businessman and my mother is an interior designer they got divorced three years back and me with my mom shifted here, also I am studying the retail management,'

'That's not your full introduction'.

'No…There is nothing much,'

'You forgot to tell me about your boyfriend '.

'Noo I don't have a boyfriend,'

'Yes you have dear, the boy who works in a hardware shop,'

'Oh my god, how do you know,'

'I know everything dear,' ' No actually he is not my boyfriend, he is my friend, actually earlier I was working in the same store, I got to know that he was dumb and deaf, once he was nearby store and someone was trying to run after looting the store, he got those people and saved the money, the store owner then offered him the job'.

'That's nice but when he is dumb and deaf, how do they communicate?'.

'Actually, the daughter of the owner is also dumb and deaf, so he knows the sign language, so It's easy for him'.

'Good, may God bless him, but are you sure you don't like him'.

'I do, but I have not told him yet'.

'Why so?'.

'I don't know how will he react?'.

'Listen, dear, when you love someone it's not always that he will be with you, but if he moves on in his life you will regret that you have not told him, so whatever the consequences would be, at least you should tell him'.

'You know you sound like a mom,' they both laughed and went back to work, Lily thought on the suggestion given by Angel. In the last week of October Lily had her birthday so she decided to tell him on that day, after Angel was leaving for home, Lily stopped her and said to her that she has decided to tell him about her feelings,' wish you a good luck dear,' ' I would be needing your help'. ' Anytime dear'.

'Thank you,' and Angel went on. After reaching home, Angel had dinner and went to bed, her eyes were wet and Shown was in front of her eyes, remembering him Angel went asleep, she saw in her dream the same boy, and he was standing in front of a photo and in that photo she saw Cory and Sophie , she woke up suddenly and was feeling anxiety , that night Angel could not sleep, she thought that he is Tyson , Angel was very angry, she was not willing to meet them but also once she wanted to know that why they abandoned her, so she decided to help Lily first and then she will meet Tyson and then through him suddenly she will appear in front of them, the next day to confirm the name of the boy , she asked lily how's Tyson, Lily said 'Tyson who?' 'You told me, the boy going to be your future boyfriend,'

'No, he is not Tyson. His name is Jerry'.

'Jerry? Where does he live, where is his family,'

'His parents stays with his brother, Jerry left his home for studying here,' Angel was thinking if he is not Tyson then who is he, still she goes for the same plan, she said,' So, what you planned for Jerry?,'

'I was thinking for a house party and then ill raise the toast and will propose him, what do you say?'.

'Chances are more than Jerry won't respond to it'.

'Why?'

'He might feel shy,'

'You suggest something good, I am terrible at planning,'

'Hmmm...You do one thing, surprise him, invite him for a house party at your place, actually there won't be a house party, only you and Jerry would be there, then you will propose him,'

'That's a good idea, thanks, now you will help me in decoration work and in gift selection,'

'For sure dear,' Lily gave Angel a tight hug and went on to their home, the next few days after work Lily and Angel went to the different places to gather decoration material and gifts for the big day while shopping Lily asked about her life while telling about her Angel broke down. Lily consoled her and suggested her to be calm and live rest of life with joy. The day before Lily's birthday she went to the place where Jerry used to work, he was there, and Lily invited her saying that there would be a house party on the birthday eve and her other friends will also come. Jerry agreed to go after he got his day off he went to a gift shop and got a beautiful watch for Lily. Jerry was feeling very happy that Lily invited him. Jerry had feelings for Lily, but he was afraid as he was Dumb and Deaf whether Lily will accept him or not. Jerry went back to his home. The next day after finishing his work he went to Lily's place, he felt something different.

He could not see any car around her place, but he moved on and ranged bell. Lily opened the door, in sign language Jerry wished her happy birthday. Lily took her in, offered him seat and said she will be back in a minute. Lily suddenly put the lights down. She got a bottle of champagne, sat beside Jerry and offered him drink.

Jerry was shy, but still he took the glass. After drink he asked Lily about her friends, she told that she invited no one else after Jerry asked why she did so. Lily got down on her knees and proposed him, Jerry got surprised and nervous. Lily judged that he is shy, so she held him and made him comfortable and told him that she loved him since the day she met him, she learned sign language to get close to him. Before she could say anything she saw that Jerry's eyes were wet and all of a sudden he tightly hugged her.

They kissed and spent a great time together, the next day Lily went early to the store and was waiting for Angel to come with Roses in her hand, as soon as Angel arrived. Lily ran towards her and hugged her tightly and started crying, Angel got worried if something went wrong, she eased her and asked her what had happened. Lily presented roses to her and said that she was pleased, and those were tears of joy, because of Angel's motivation only she got her life's biggest happiness.

Angel understood that Jerry and Lily were in relation now, Angel got that as an opportunity, she invited Lily and Jerry for dinner to celebrate. She agreed on behalf of Jerry as well, the same evening when Lily met Jerry she told her about the invitation and also that she agreed on his behalf as well, so for the next evening, they gathered at the restaurant decided, there they had introduction and Angel was able to ask for the address where Jerry's parents reside. She got to know that they were living in Austin, after dinner while going back to the place, Angel was thinking how she could see them, that time Angel was back into memories with Sophie and Cory and was feeling pain why they abandoned her at that time when she was ill. After 3 days Lily told Angel at work that she and Jerry have decided to visit Austin to see Jerry's parents and after that they will get married. Angel got an idea and asked Angel in a sarcastic way,' Would I be invited in your marriage'.

'Of course, without you my marriage is incomplete,' Angel got that day as a chance to come in front of Cory and Sophie, that day when Angel reached home she got to know that Aunty Shania was hospitalized, she got swelling in her brain and was left with very less time, Angel reached there and luckily she was alive when Angel arrived there , she took her hand said ,' Aunty I am here'.

'I know dear, but I have very less time to be with, just wanted to say make your mind and soul be in rest, don't get distressed,'

'I'll do, aunty you will be fine don't worry,'

'I know my life dear, but I have seen some restlessness in you,' All of a sudden Aunty felt blank, nurse suddenly called doctor, and he said she has gone paralysed, Angel felt very bad, everyone from home was there and they sent her back home as she had to go to work and assured her if something is needed they will call her back, she went back to home before going to bed she was thinking of Aunty Shania and prayed for her good health, as soon as she got asleep she had a dream that Aunty Shania was there in front of her and came closer, she said 'Ask my child what you want to know'.

'How do you know I wanted to ask something,'

'I can read it on your face, dear,'

'Aunty if I could not come to you when you are not well, would you be angry from me?'

'Probably not because I know you love me and you might be busy somewhere,' 'is it so easy to say this'.

'Dear first thing is if you have not done anything wrong to another person and then he abandons you. Possibilities are that he might be in some problem, but still, he abandons you intentionally then you should have a forgiving nature,' just after this Angel's phone rang 7 she woke up, it was call from hospital that Aunty Shania passed away. Angel got very sad, she cried 7 then rushed towards hospital. On the way she thought that the words she got from Aunty Shania were important. She should also think about forgiving Cory and Sophie. Day after funeral of Aunty Shania she got a call from Lily, and she gave her the good news that next week in Austin. Jerry and Lily would get married, and Angel has to come for the occasion. Angel with a forgiving mind decides to visit there and meet everyone.

The next weekday before marriage, Angel reached there and called Lilly. She came along with Jerry to pick her from the airport. On the way to Jerry's home, Lilly was telling everything about the arrangements etc, but Angel was having something else in her mind also she was nervous. Was thinking that what will they talk about, as soon as they reached home. Cory and Sophie were there in the living room Lilly, and Jerry introduced Angel to Cory and Sophie. They both got shocked to see Angel, tears went upon their eyes. Before Cory and Sophie could say anything Angel hugged them tightly and started crying Lilly and Jerry were not able to understand that why they were crying.

Before asking anything they made everyone comfortable gave them water, Sophie and Cory apologized for not coming to her. Jerry signed to Sophie that how she knew Angel, Cory looked towards Sophie. She nodded her head to yes and then Cory revealed that Jerry was the Son of Angel.

By this Angel got shocked meanwhile Lilly in sign language told Jerry that Angel was his mom, Sophie held Angel's hand and told her ,' After that accident you got into coma but by the will of god Jerry or you can say Shown survived but due to that accident he lost his ability to talk and listen, thereafter me and Cory decided to leave the city so that we could bring Jerry(Shown) and no complications are there…I have treated him as my own son and see the fortune on the big day of your son, you are here…I am Sorry,'

Jerry came towards Angel and Angel kissed his forehead and gave him a tight hug, then she turned towards Lilly. She hugged her and thanked her because of her only Angel reunited with her son. All of a sudden Jerry (Shown) cried loudly, and Lilly asked him why he was crying like that. Jerry (Shown)said something in sign language and Lilly also got sad, then she told everyonc that he was now confused whom to say mom, both Angel and Sophie came closer and gave him a tight hug and Angel said that you are the luckiest person in the world who has 2 moms.

Jerry (Shown) signed that he could not understand and smile a bit, Lilly translated in sign language. And he hugged tightly everyone, the next day his marriage took place Lilly came to Angel and said that I got my best friend as my mother now. With Jerry I am also the luckiest ones, that evening, Angel packed her bags and was about to go, but all of them insisted on staying with them. Finally she agreed to stay with them. She saw Lilly and Jerry before going to bed and slept deep, soon after she slept.

She saw Emma calling her, in her dream, she found herself as a child and Emma waiting for her on dining table with pancakes. She ran towards her and started having treated with Emma. Emma cried with a smile and said 'My child it's time to come with me, **THE CHASE OF DREAMS** has finally ended for you,'…